On the Banks of the Hudson

On the Banks
of the Hudson

A View of its History and Folklore

Beman Lord

Illustrated by Rocco Negri

Henry Z. Walck, Inc.
New York

Copyright © 1971 by Beman Lord
Illustrations copyright © 1971 by Rocco Negri
All rights reserved
ISBN: 0–8098–2075–7
Library of Congress Catalog Card Number: 75–142451
Printed in the United States of America

To Refna

Contents

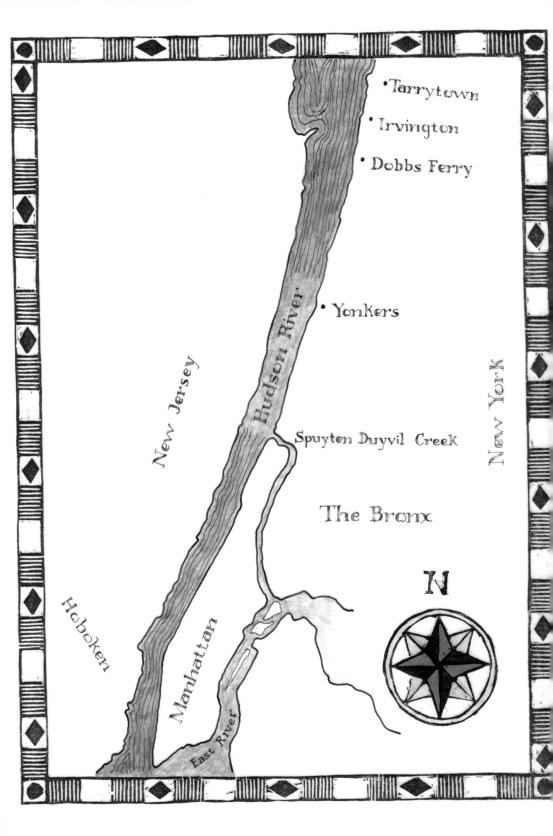

I

New York

The Hudson was probably first discovered by an Italian, Giovanni da Verrazano who was sailing for the French. This was in 1524 when he found New York Harbor and started to explore the great river, but a storm came up and he had to leave the area. A year later a Portuguese, Estevan Gómez, sailing for Spain made a map of the coastal area from Connecticut to Delaware but he did not explore any of the rivers. It wasn't until 1609 that an Englishman, Henry Hudson, sailing for the Dutch explored the river all the way up to Albany. He did not find the Northwest Passage to China which he was searching for but he found a beautiful river and a fertile valley.

It is estimated that there were over 20,000 Indians living along its banks. The Algonquins and the Mohicans occupied both sides of the river south of Albany; the Delawares were on the west shore below Catskill to New Jersey. The Wappingers were on the east side from Poughkeepsie south to Manhattan. The Montauks were on the island and in Brooklyn.

Hudson and his mate, Robert Juet, made an experiment to see if some of the Indians were friendly or treacherous. They got them drunk with wine. After the Indians watched the zigzag effect of the liquor on their brothers, they were sure that the river must have gotten drunk at one time to have such a zigzag channel to the sea. From that time on they searched for the fountain of "fire water" without any luck.

It wasn't until the last three days of the expedition that there was any trouble with the Indians. An Indian had been following the ship the *Half Moon* as it sailed down the river. When he saw his chance, he climbed on board and stole Robert Juet's pillow, some shirts and belts. Mr. Juet saw him and shot him dead. The next day the Indians sought revenge. They sent war canoes and shot arrows at the ship as it sailed down to Manhattan. The next day the *Half Moon* left for Holland, after spending a month on the river.

Several years later Hudson was still trying to find the Northwest Passage and had sailed into Hudson Bay. From November to the early summer the ship was locked in ice. After this long delay the crew insisted on returning home. There was only enough bread to last them a few weeks, but fish was plentiful and Hudson wanted to push on. The sailors mutinied and set Hudson and his son and a few others adrift in a boat. They were never heard from again. One of the men to turn against Hudson was Robert Juet.

The *Half Moon* returned to Holland and word spread of the great country across the sea. A group of colonists set sail from the city of Amsterdam to the shores of America. The ship was called the *Goede Vrouw* or "good woman." The voyage was very pleasant and the Dutch thought it was due to the blessings and care of St. Nicholas. The ship landed at the mouth of the Hudson.

Here, lifting up their eyes, so the story goes, they beheld a small Indian village on what is at present called the Jersey shore. The natives collected on the beach, gazing in stunned admiration at the *Goede Vrouw*. A boat was immediately sent from the ship to enter into a treaty with them. As the Dutch approached the shore, they hailed them through a trumpet in the most friendly terms. The Indians were so confounded at the sound of the Dutch language, that they all took to their heels and scampered over the Bergen hills. They didn't stop until they had buried themselves, head and ears, in the New Jersey marshes where they all perished to a man.

The valiant heroes sprang ashore in triumph and took possession of the land as conquerors in the

name of their country and entered the village of Communipaw, defended only by a few old squaws and papooses. On looking about them they were so overjoyed that they were sure that the blessed St. Nicholas had guided them to this place as the spot to settle. The present-day site would be somewhere between Hoboken and Amboy.

One day while exploring the river, a group was washed up on the island in the bay. As the tide was too great to make it to their village, they had to spend the night. It was here that Oloffe Van Kortlandt had his dream.

Oloffe dreamed that the good St. Nicholas came riding over the trees in the same sled that he brings his Christmas presents in to children. He landed by the fire where the people of Communipaw had cooked their supper. He lit his pipe from the fire and sat himself down and smoked. The smoke rose in the air and spread like a cloud overhead. Oloffe climbed the tallest tree and saw that the smoke spread over the island and looked like tall spires and steeples. When St. Nicholas had smoked his pipe, he laid his finger beside his nose and gave the astonished Oloffe a very significant look, mounted his sled and rode away over the treetops. After Oloffe awoke, he roused his companions and told them his dream. It was the will of St. Nicholas, he said, that they should settle here and the smoke of his pipe showed how big and tall the city would be. They would call it New Amsterdam. The river would be the Mauritius, named after the good prince of Holland.

The city grew and in 1641 there were 2,000 homes. In 1664 a fleet of five British vessels appeared in New Amsterdam Harbor and took over the Dutch colony. King Charles II of England, without telling the Dutch, gave all the Dutch land in America to his brother, the Duke of York.

Governor Peter Stuyvesant, when he saw the ships, called on his right-hand man, Anthony Van Corlear, to summon help from the land up the river—Tarrytown, Petticoat-Lane, Sleepy Hollow, the Bronx. Anthony, stopping only to eat a large dinner and take a few swigs from his faithful bottle, ran from the city gates, sounding a farewell blast from his trumpet.

It was a dark and stormy night when the good Anthony arrived at the creek which separated the island from the mainland. The wind was high and the elements were in an uproar, and no boatman could be found to take him across the creek. For a short time he paused on the edge. Then he remembered the urgency of his errand and, taking a few more swigs from his bottle, swore that he would swim across in spite of the devil. He daringly plunged into the stream. Luckless Anthony! Scarcely had he gotten halfway over, when he started to struggle violently, as if battling with the devil of the waters. Instinctively he put his trumpet to his mouth and, giving a strong blast, sank forever to the bottom.

The noise of his trumpet rang far and wide through the country, alarming the neighbors

round, who hurried in amazement to the spot. Here an old Dutchman, who had witnessed the sad affair, swore that he had seen the devil, in the shape of a huge fish, seize Anthony by the legs and drag him beneath the waves. That is why it is called Spuyten Duyvil Creek even to this day. Some say that the ghost of poor Anthony still haunts the area and his trumpet can be heard on dark and stormy nights. A toll bridge has now been built there as an exit from Manhattan so that there won't be any more accidents with the devil. It is easier to pay a few cents toll than to take a chance of meeting that beast.

Whether Anthony would have changed history if he had gotten word to the Dutch in time to stop the British from taking over the New Netherlands colonies, is anyone's guess. In any case, nothing much changed except the names. New Amsterdam became New York, Wiltwyck became Kingston and the river of Prince Mauritius became the Hudson.

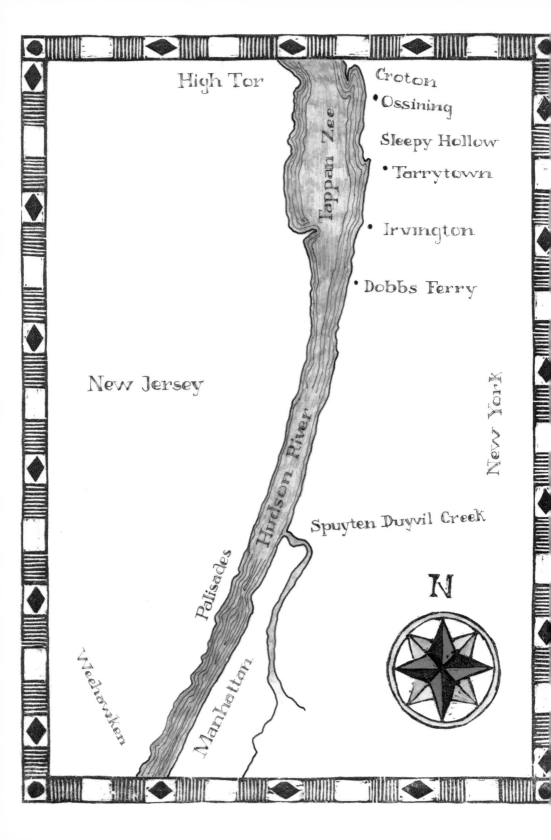

2

Tappan Zee

Across the river at Weehawken is where the Palisades begin and continue for about twenty miles up the river to the Tappan Zee. They are huge cliffs dropping to the river and the name Palisades means "logs set on end." Their height starts at about three hundred feet and gradually rises to a height of five hundred and fifty feet. This front of solid rock separates the valleys of the Hudson and Hackensack rivers, which flow parallel for thirty miles. It is said that the Indian Great Spirit built this wall to keep out man from his favorite Hudson valley.

Weehawken was where the famous duel between Aaron Burr and Alexander Hamilton took place. Burr, who was vice-president of the United States, had run for governor of New York State and had lost. He accused Hamilton of writing some speeches criticizing him and challenged him to a duel. On July 11, 1804 both men rowed across the river and climbed up the cliffs to a small landing. It has been said that Hamilton fired in the air and Burr took deadly aim. In any case, Hamilton died the next day. Burr was charged with murder but the case never went to trial. He was later tried for treason but was found not guilty.

Just a few miles above Spuyten Duyvil Creek stands the city of Yonkers. When the Dutch first came to settle along the Hudson, one could buy large pieces of land from the Dutch government. A young Dutch lord bought the Yonkers area. In Dutch it was called the "Colony of the Jonkeer's," meaning his young lordship. Eventually he returned to Holland and sold the land to Frederick Philipse. In 1813 most of the city and area, three hundred and twenty acres, was sold at auction for

$56,000. Today, a little over 150 years later, it is the fourth largest city in the state.

Farther up the river we come to the Tappan Zee. Tappan means "cold springs." Here the river is at its widest, three and a half miles at one point.

Rambout Van Dam, who lived at Spuyten Duyvil, heard that there was going to be a party in one of the villages on the banks of the Tappan Zee. He rowed all the way up the river and apparently did not find this pull very tiring for he danced and out-drank everyone at the party.

It was a Saturday night and twelve o'clock came before he realized the time. Then he started for home. His companions warned him against the perils of Sabbath-breaking which was considered a serious sin. But Rambout was confident and reckless and disregarded every warning. He set off in his boat saying he would not land until he reached his home at Spuyten Duyvil. He has not arrived there yet. Because of his breaking the

Sunday laws, he is doomed to journey on the broad river until the day of judgment. Often in the still twilight of a summer evening, when the opposite hills throw their purple shadows half across the river, the steady pulling of oars can be heard, though not a boat can be seen.

Perhaps Rambout was visiting at Dobbs Ferry which was named after a Swedish ferryman, Jeremiah Dobbs. Some called it Weeckqualsquck, which was probably the Indian name. Many citizens wanted to change the name. They didn't like Dobbs or Weeckqualsquck. They wanted to call it after a Revolutionary hero, Van Wart. Someone suggested that they drop the "Van" and call the place "Wart on the Hudson."

Above Dobbs Ferry is the town of Irvington named after the famous writer, Washington Irving. Some of the stories in this book are from his writings. Perhaps his most famous is the story of the headless horseman, "The Legend of Sleepy Hollow," which took place in Tarrytown.

In the village lived a poor schoolmaster, Ichabod Crane, whom everyone liked. With very good luck, he fell in love with a rich young girl, Katrina Van Tassel, whose father owned a large farm. However, Brom Van Brunt, the hero of the country round, also had decided to marry Katrina. A feud developed between the two men.

One night both men were invited to a party at the Van Tassels'. Ichabod borrowed from his neighbor a horse named Gunpowder. Brom rode his own horse, Daredevil, a creature like himself.

After eating and dancing, both men joined a group who were telling stories. Naturally, the headless horseman was discussed. Brom then boasted that one night when returning from the nearby village of Sing Sing, he had been overtaken by the rider and they had a race. He could have beaten him, he said, but when they came to the church bridge, the horseman vanished in a flash of fire.

As the party broke up, Ichabod lingered behind to speak to Katrina. No one knows what happened but when Ichabod left, he was sad and crestfallen. He was more interested in the money than in the girl and it seemed now that all his dreams of wealth might not come true. On his way home all the stories of ghosts and goblins kept running through his mind, especially the one about the headless horseman. The night grew darker and darker as he approached the place where many of the stories had taken place. He tried to whistle to give himself courage. As he approached a stream, his heart began to thump, and he urged his horse to go faster. The horse suddenly stopped and Ichabod was almost thrown over his head. Just at this moment a noise was heard. Ichabod looked and saw something huge, misshapen, black and towering. It was like a gigantic monster ready to spring upon him.

The hair of Ichabod's head rose with terror. What was to be done? To turn and fly was now too late; and besides, what chance was there of escaping ghost or goblin? Suddenly the shape moved into the middle of the road. He appeared to be a huge horseman on a big black horse. Ichabod was sure that the horseman's head, which should have been on his shoulders, was carried before him on the saddle.

There then began a chase over the countryside as Ichabod tried to flee from this strange midnight companion. Ichabod's fear had spread to his horse as Ichabod spurred him faster and faster. Suddenly his saddle broke and Ichabod clung to the horse's

neck. Up ahead he could see the church bridge where the demon should disappear. He urged the horse faster and finally crossed the bridge. Ichabod looked behind to see if his pursuer would vanish, but just then the rider rose in his stirrups and hurled his head at Ichabod. Ichabod tried to dodge it, but it caught him and he fell from the horse.

The next morning the old horse was found without a saddle, but Ichabod was never seen again. Near the church bridge was found a broken pumpkin.

Brom married Katrina. It was said that when Brom heard the story told later about Ichabod's disappearance that he looked very knowingly and burst into a hearty laugh at the mention of the pumpkin.

Just above Tarrytown is Ossining. The Indians named it Sing Sing which means, "rocky nature of the site." Here is where the famous prison is located. In 1901, the people of the town grew tired of all the jokes connected with their village and the prison and changed the name from Sing Sing to Ossining. The prison also changed its name.

On the same side of the river, at Croton, stood the manor house of the Van Cortlandts. It is haunted by an Indian ghost, Chief Croton. It was here that the Chief made a desperate last stand against enemies from the north. He fought with great courage amid a shower of arrows and half-hidden by the smoke and flames of his burning fort. One by one his tribesmen fell, till he stood alone and wounded. Then, as his foes rushed forward, he fell headlong on the blazing fire. He died, yet it is said that in great trouble he comes forward and urges men to courageous deeds.

Across the river is High Tor. Long ago a wise man from the East found his way to America and on the top of High Tor he built an altar. This angered the Indians and they demanded that he worship as they did. When he refused, they decided to kill him. The man was saved by a miracle, for an earthquake opened a great crack in the earth and swallowed all the Indians. This crack, of course, became the channel through which the Hudson now flows.

Another mountain stands nearby. It is called Treason Hill. This was the place where General Benedict Arnold of the American forces during the American Revolution plotted with Major John André of the British army. General Arnold had sought and obtained from General Washington the important military post at West Point. He planned to turn the fort over to the British. Because he had not received proper recognition fighting for the Americans and had married a woman whose father supported the British, Arnold was going to turn traitor.

Arnold gave André papers outlining the plan. The ship which was to take André back to New York had been fired upon by the Americans and had to leave the area. Therefore, André crossed the river at Kings Ferry and continued on land towards New York. Near Tarrytown, he met three men. One was wearing a Hessian uniform. As the Hessians were on the side of the British, André asked for help. That was his mistake, for the men were Americans and the one wearing the uniform had just escaped from the British in that disguise. Arnold escaped to England but Major André was tried by a military court and was hanged. It is said that on the day Arnold died, lightning struck and burned the tree where André was captured.

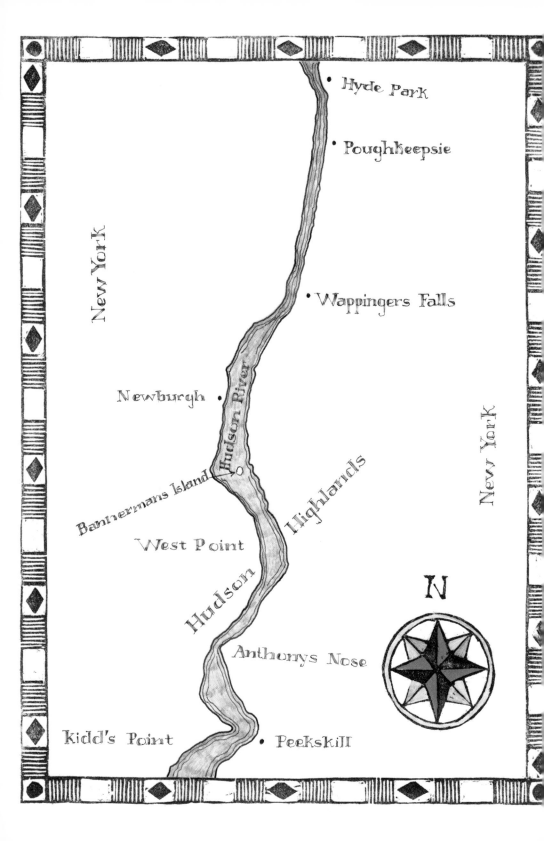

3

The Highlands and Hillsides

On the west bank of the Hudson across from Peekskill is Kidd's Point. Captain Kidd was, of course, a pirate. After capturing several ships in the West Indies, he divided the treasure with his crew. Captain Kidd sailed away in one ship while most of his crew went in another. The crew wanted to return to the Highlands of the Hudson where they lived. Almost home, they encountered a gale and, thinking they were being followed, ran the ship near the shore and sank her. The crew fled to the woods, leaving the treasure to sink to the bottom. Many people have tried to find it since but have been unsuccessful. Perhaps it is still there.

A few miles upstream is Anthonys Nose on one

side and Fort Clinton on the other. Some say Anthonys Nose is named after the famous trumpeter from New Amsterdam. Fort Clinton was one of the American forts during the Revolution. During the war, the Americans placed a 1500-foot chain across the river between these two points. It was to keep the British from coming up the river. Part of Arnold's plan was that under pretense of having the chain repaired, one link was to be taken out for a few days and rope put in its place. This would be easily broken by the ships. The plan failed when André was captured, but eventually the British did come up the river. They captured Fort Clinton and cut the chain. It took them almost twelve hours to do so, however.

Later on another chain was placed across the river from West Point to Constitution Bay. It was 1700 feet long, weighed 180 tons, and each link was two feet, nine inches long. If you ever visit West Point, you will be able to see some of the chain.

West Point became a military academy on July 4, 1802. It opened with ten cadets and since that time has turned out numerous great generals—Lee, Grant, MacArthur, Eisenhower, to name a few.

Near West Point is the deepest part of the river, just over two hundred feet.

Just below Newburgh is Bannermans Island. It used to be called Pollopel's Island named after Polly Pell. Polly had two suitors after her hand. One was a minister and one was a farmer. One winter night the minister took her for a sleigh ride. On the river, near the island, the ice broke and they were plunged into the cold freezing water. The farmer happened to be not too far away and came and rescued them. Polly at once embraced her rescuer with great warmth. She tried to get as close as possible to the farmer. The minister saw this and realized that he had lost out to the farmer. He promptly married them in the moonlight.

When Robert Juet of the *Half Moon* saw the

spot where Newburgh now stands, he said, "That would be a very pleasant place to build a town." It was settled much later by a group of settlers from Germany who were brought to this country by the British government. It was here that the American army camped for two years after the Revolutionary War had ended, waiting for the peace terms to be settled. Washington had his headquarters here at several times, and it was where he received a letter from a group of officers asking him to become king. He refused this honor immediately.

Back across the river is Poughkeepsie. Here was where the vote was taken for New York State to become one of the thirteen states. It was decided to do so by only one vote on July 26, 1788. The Indians called it Apo Keep Sinck—"safe harbor."

An Indian warrior from the Pequod tribe was captured by the Delawares, who lived on the other side of the river. He was taken back to their tribe and was offered his freedom if he would renounce his own tribe and join theirs. He refused and was bound to a tree for sacrifice. His maiden had followed him and entered the camp. She pleaded to the Delawares for his life. As the Indians were talking it over, they were attacked by some Hurons. In the confusion, the maiden untied her lover and they escaped. However, they became separated and she was captured by the Hurons. This time he rescued her and they escaped across the river. The strong arms of the young warrior paddled his loved one safely to a deep rocky nook north of a creek where they hid. The Hurons set off after them but were sent back across the river by the warrior's tribe. The nook was indeed a "safe harbor."

Above Poughkeepsie is Hyde Park where President Franklin D. Roosevelt was born and is buried. The house is still like it was in his time with a museum and library attached.

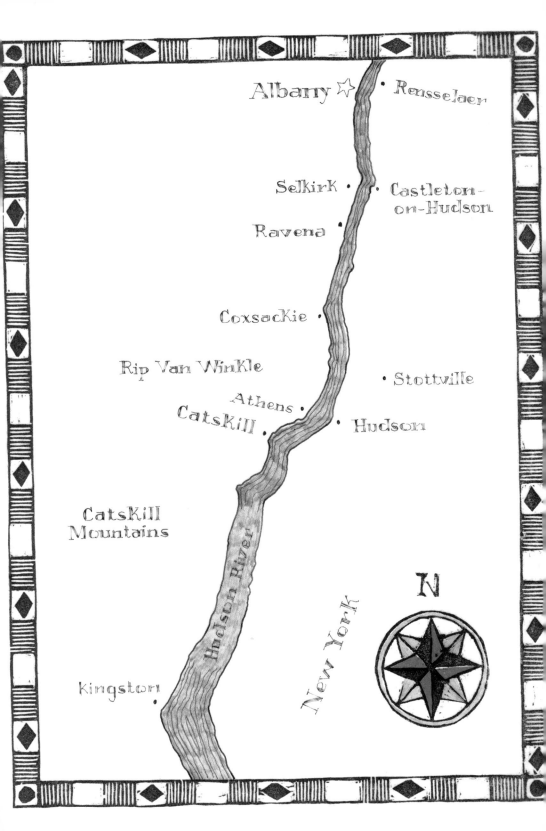

4

The Catskills

In the Mountains of the Sky, or the Onteoras as
the Indians called them, lived an old squaw spirit.
She was in charge of the great treasury of storm
and sunshine for the region. She dwelt on the
highest peak of the mountains and she kept day
and night shut up in her wigwam, letting out only
one at a time. She made new moons every month
and hung them up in the sky, cutting up the old
ones into stars. The Great Manitow, or master
spirit, employed her to manufacture clouds. Sometimes she wove them out of cobwebs, gossamers
and morning dew and sent them off flake after
flake to float in the air and give light summer
showers. Sometimes she would brew up black

thunderstorms to swell the streams. Sometimes she would shut the winds up in the caverns of the hills.

Kingston has had many names—Esopus, Rondout, Wiltwyck, Swanenburgh. The present name was given to it by an English governor who called it after his home in England, Kingston L'Isle. The village was twice destroyed by Indians before the Revolution. This was the farthest point Sir Henry Clinton of the British army came up the river after he had broken through the chain. He burned Kingston to the ground leaving only one barn and one house standing. The courthouse at Kingston was where the first state constitution was adopted, where the first governor was sworn in, and where the first legislature met. There is a museum now which you can visit. It is fireproof.

At Tivoli was the estate of Robert Livingston. It was his money that enabled Robert Fulton to build his first steamboat and he named it after Livingston's house, Clermont. Everyone called it

"Fulton's Folly." When it came time for the trial run in New York City, no one would ride on it. One of my great-great-grandfathers was going to Columbia University and he along with some other medical students took the first ride. Shortly after that, in 1807, it made the trip from New York City to Albany in thirty-two hours. One of the farmers, as he watched it going up the river, said he had seen the devil going up the river in a sawmill. The steamboat changed the whole life of the river as goods could now move quickly up and down the river.

In the village of Catskill lived a good-natured farmer by the name of Rip Van Winkle. Everyone loved him, especially the children. He would tell them stories of ghosts, witches and Indians. He would play their favorite games. The only fault that could be found with Rip was that he didn't like to work.

"How can you be a farmer and not work?" his

wife would ask, and nag him from morning till night. Rip would shrug his shoulders and say nothing. Even Rip's dog was nagged at so that when he entered the house, his tail drooped to the ground or curled between his legs. Wolf was always on the lookout for Dame Van Winkle's broom which would come flying at him.

The only way for Rip and Wolf to escape from the nagging and farm work was to take to the hills. One day while out hunting, Rip had climbed to one of the highest parts of the Catskill Mountains. He realized that night was coming and he would not make it home in time for supper. As he was about to climb down and hurry home, he heard a voice. "Rip Van Winkle! Rip Van Winkle!" He looked around but could see nothing except a crow winging its solitary flight across the mountains. He thought he must be hearing things and turned again to go down. The cry came again, "Rip Van Winkle! Rip Van Winkle!" Wolf heard it too, for he let out a growl and hurried

to his master's side. Rip now began to get wor-
ried. He looked again in the direction of the sound
and saw a strange figure coming up the rocks,
bending under the weight of something he carried
on his back. Rip was surprised to see someone in
this lonely place and, supposing it was someone
from the neighborhood in need of assistance, hast-
ened down to help.

When Rip got closer he was still more surprised
at the stranger's appearance. He was a short, old
fellow with thick bushy hair and a grizzled beard
and dressed in the old Dutch fashion. On his
shoulder was a keg that seemed full of liquor. He
motioned to Rip to come and help him with the
keg. Together they climbed up the mountain in
silence until they reached a level spot where a
group of men were bowling. They were dressed
in the same way as the stranger and did not speak.
The stranger opened the keg and drinks were
passed around. Rip had more than his share and
eventually fell into a deep sleep.

On waking it was a bright sunny morning.
Surely, he thought, I have not slept here all night.
That liquor! That wicked liquor! What excuse
shall I make to Dame Van Winkle!

He looked around for his gun, but in place of
his clean well-oiled one, he found an old rusted

musket by him. Wolf too had disappeared. He whistled for him and shouted his name, but no dog was to be seen. As he rose to walk, he found himself stiff in the joints and without much energy. What was to be done? He was hungry for breakfast but he hated to leave his gun and dog. Also his wife would be angry if he didn't get home soon. He started for home.

As he approached the village he met a number of people but none whom he knew, which surprised him for he had thought he knew everyone in the village. Their dress was of a different fashion and all the people stared at him and stroked their chins. Rip touched his chin and to his astonishment found his beard had grown a foot long!

When he reached his house the roof had fallen in, the windows were shuttered, doors were off the hinges, and it was empty. He hurried to the village inn and found that that had changed also. A crowd soon gathered around to look at him and asked questions of what he was doing in their

village. Rip said he was looking for his old friends and, on naming them, learned that they were all dead. In despair, he cried out, "Does anyone here know Rip Van Winkle?"

"Oh, Rip Van Winkle," they answered. "That's Rip leaning against the tree."

Rip looked and saw that the man looked exactly as he had looked when he had gone up the mountain the day before. "Does anyone know *old* Rip Van Winkle?" he asked.

All stood amazed, until an old woman came and looked closely at Rip. "Sure enough. It is Rip Van Winkle—it is himself! Welcome home again old neighbor. Where have you been these twenty long years?"

There is another tale that is not in Washington Irving's story. It seems that when Rip woke up he looked for his dog for he had tied him to a small tree when he went to sleep. Now he found a big tree and, looking up, saw the bones of his dog tied to one of the branches.

On the other side of the river is Hudson. At one time this town grew more rapidly than any other town in America except Baltimore. It became an important whaling seaport and had more sailing vessels than New York City. It almost became the capital of the state but lost by one vote to Albany.

Near the city is a small island called Noah's Brig. One night a raft under command of a man whose first name was Noah neared this point and saw a dark object looming before him. He thought it was a ship under full sail.

"Ship ahoy," he shouted.

There was no answer. Again in a strong voice he hailed the craft and still received no answer. The mysterious vessel kept unswervingly to its course. Noah was exasperated and he yelled, "Ahoy there! Answer or I'll run you down!"

No reply came, and, true to his word, he ran down the island. What he thought were two masts and sails proved to be tall trees.

5

Albany and the Headwaters

In 1624 eighteen families sailed up the river as far as they could go. They established Fort Orange, named after the ruling house in Holland. There had been an earlier fort built in 1614 but that had been abandoned. In 1686 it became the first American city under a charter of the English governor. For the payment of one beaver skin a year, Albany had control of the fur trade. This enabled Albany to become prosperous and grow. It became the state capital in 1797.

Baas Volckert Jan Pietersen Van Amsterdam owned a bake shop in Albany. He invented New Year cakes and gingerbread babies. One day an ugly old woman entered his shop.

"Give me a dozen New Year cookies," she said in a shrill voice.

"Well, you needn't speak so loud," Baas answered. "I ain't deaf."

He gave her the cookies. She counted them. "A dozen," she screamed. "Give me a dozen. You have only given me twelve."

"Well, twelve is a dozen," he answered.

"One more. I want a dozen!"

"Well, if you want another, go to the devil and get it."

The woman left and from then on there was nothing but trouble in the shop. Cakes were stolen, his bread was either too heavy or too light, his wife became deaf, and business became very bad. Twice the woman came back and demanded another cookie. Twice he sent her away. Finally he called on St. Nicholas to help him.

"Be more generous," St. Nick said. "Give her one more." He vanished and the woman appeared. The baker gave her one more cookie.

"The spell is broken," she said. "From this time

57

on twelve is thirteen." So until thirteen new states rose from the ruins of the colonies and became shrewd Yankees, a baker's dozen was always thirteen. However, there are still some bakery shops today where you can get an extra cookie for your dozen.

Sam Wilson was a Troy meatpacker and supplied the army of 1812 with meat. He stamped his products U.S. One of his workmen said it stood for Uncle Sam. The joke must have been taken up by others for today we all know that U.S. stands for Uncle Sam as well as the United States.

One of the most important battles in the Revolution took place near Saratoga. The British planned to separate the colonies by controlling the Hudson River. An army would come up from the south and General Burgoyne from the north. Burgoyne's advance from Canada up Lake Champlain and capturing Fort Ticonderoga had been easy. However, the Americans put up a strong fight under General Gates and defeated Burgoyne.

General Clinton by this time was burning Kingston, and when he heard the news of the defeat, returned to New York. General Benedict Arnold, before he was commander at West Point, played an important part in the battle. With this victory the Americans stopped an important part of the British army, captured valuable military supplies, and did not allow the British to separate the colonies. It also convinced the French to come to the aid of the Americans.

In the vicinity of Saratoga, a young Mohawk lost his way. In vain he wandered day after day in darkness trying to find his way out of the forest. He believed that he was being led round and round in a circle until in the center would be death. Finally when he was almost starved and frantic, a large gray owl flew across his path. Turning its big staring eyes at the Indian, it said, "To whoo! To whoo! It is I who have bound thee in my spell. It is I who have wound you round and round the charmed circle. It is I who with my wife

and children in yonder hollow tree will fatten off thy flesh. To whoo! To whoo! It is time for thee to die! To whoo! To whoo!"

The Mohawk, using his last strength, raised his bow and let fly an arrow which brought the monster to the ground. Exhausted by his effort, he leaned against a tree and looked at the dead bird. From its body flew forth a beautiful white dove. Immediately the clouds which had covered the sky broke away and the full moon rose in the east. The dove flew before the hunter as if inviting him to follow her. He did, and it fluttered along before him till it led him to safety.

Glens Falls was known as Che-pon-tuc, "a hard place to get around." A Mr. Wing owned the region and the falls were known as Wings Falls. Mr. Wing sold the right to the name to a Mr. Glen for the price of a dinner at the tavern. After Mr. Glen had paid for the meal, he posted on all the roads around the falls its new name—Glens Falls.

On the highest mountain of the state, Mt. Marcy, is a two-acre pond known as Lake Tear of the Clouds. This is the beginning of the river and it is from here that the river starts its 306-mile trip to the sea. I know it has more stories to tell but that will have to wait for another time.

Afterword

I am extremely indebted to the New York Public Library where all my research took place. I have used many books, but the following were my main sources:

Bacon, Edgar M. *Hudson River from Ocean to Source.* New York and London: G. P. Putnam's Sons, 1902.

Bruce, Wallace. *The Hudson.* New York: Bryant Union, 1907.

Johnson, Clifton. *The Picturesque Hudson.* New York: Macmillan, 1909.

Skinner, Charles M. *Myths and Legends of Our Own Land.* 2 vols. Philadelphia and London: J. B. Lippincott, 1896.

Probably these books will not be found in your library as they are very old and valuable. However, you will find the works of Washington Irving and, if you would like to read more stories about the river, I suggest Carl Carmer's *The Hudson*, published in New York and Toronto by Farrar & Rinehart, 1939.

No book on the Hudson would be complete without the tales of Washington Irving, and I hope he will forgive my brevity in retelling some of them.

I apologize to all the communities along the Hudson that I have quickly skipped over or have omitted. My purpose was to give a flavor and some of the history of this wonderful river.